HUNTED

OUTRUN. OUTLAST. OUTWIT.

Tales Of Adventure

Edited By Jenni Harrison

First published in Great Britain in 2020 by:

Young Writers
Remus House
Coltsfoot Drive
Peterborough
PE2 9BF
Telephone: 01733 890066
Website: www.youngwriters.co.uk

Book Design by Ashley Janson

Softback ISBN 978-1-83928-428-1

Printed and bound in the UK by BookPrintingUK
Website: www.bookprintinguk.com
YB0438Q

FOREWORD

IF YOU'VE BEEN SEARCHING FOR EPIC ADVENTURES, TALES OF SUSPENSE AND IMAGINATIVE WRITING THEN SEARCH NO MORE! YOUR HUNT IS AT AN END WITH THIS ANTHOLOGY OF MINI SAGAS.

We challenged secondary school students to craft a story in just 100 words. In this first installment of our SOS Sagas, their mission was to write on the theme of 'Hunted'. But they weren't restricted to just predator vs prey, oh no. They were encouraged to think beyond their first instincts and explore deeper into the theme.

The result is a variety of styles and genres and, as well as some classic cat and mouse games, inside these pages you'll find characters looking for meaning, people running from their darkest fears or maybe even death itself on the hunt.

Here at Young Writers it's our aim to inspire the next generation and instill in them a love for creative writing, and what better way than to see their work in print? The imagination and skill within these pages are proof that we might just be achieving that aim! Well done to each of these fantastic authors.

So if you're ready to find out if the hunter will become the hunted, read on!

CONTENTS

Bishopton Centre, Billingham

Liam Bray (13) 1
Ryan Robert Briggs (13) 2

Rivers Education Support Centre, Hoddesdon

Paul Nathan Parewa (12) 3
Charlie Curtis (14) 4
Divine Ephraim (14) 5
Lennon Pearse (13) 6

Shire Oak Academy, Walsall Wood

Sarah Bissaker 7
Grace Simmons 8
Daisy Reynolds (12) 9
Kat Zachariou 10
Alexandra Peat (13) 11
Ruby May Howell (13) 12
Iman Sajjad Bhatti (11) 13
Emma Feilden (13) 14
Eric Hikins (12) 15
Nicole Nayler (12) 16
Harvey Bird 17
Josh Turner 18
Zak Moulick (12) 19
Ava Webb (11) 20
Abby Gray 21
Chelsie Cox (13) 22
Bradley Green (15) 23
Alexander Andrew Walker (12) 24
Charlie Hems 25
Amelia-Rose Price (13) 26
Campbell Smith (11) 27
Kylan Bullock (11) 28
Aleesha Scarlet Barrier (11) 29
Paige Dunning (13) 30
Mai Jones 31
Yvie Mae Bowler (12) 32
Connor Ray Lemord (13) 33
Ruby Grace Walklate (12) 34
Lucy Heeley 35
Jack Clarke (11) 36
Harry Ttiniozou 37
Yazmin Tolley 38
Mollie Taylor 39
Emily Brabbin 40
Varia Daro Aziz (12) 41
Ethan Clarke (12) 42
Olly Foster 43
Eloise Peach 44
Millie Spruce (13) 45
Zak Charles Carley (11) 46
Christopher Pedley (13) 47
Isla McCullagh 48
Mayson Joynes (13) 49
Maisie Elizabeth Andrews (16) 50
KJ Parton 51
Eva Webster 52
Olivia Sturch 53
Lydia Scott 54
Molly Ivins (12) 55
Paige Startup 56
Alicia Heath 57
Zoe Tolley 58
Kyle Luke Chambers (12) 59
Callum Sedgwick 60
Sophie Eloise Webb (12) 61

Ciaran Yates 62
Mitchell Meeson 63
Evie Wilson (12) 64
Emily Jackson (14) 65
Tyler Adam Roden (13) 66

St Cuthbert's Catholic High School, Newcastle Upon Tyne

Samuel Vincent (12) 67
Ashtone Noel Hindes (12) 68
Hussain Jabar (13) 69
James Dann (12) 70
Hasib Younis 71
Phillipe Coloma 72

St John Baptist CIW High School, Aberdare

Zachary Phillips-Sinigoj (12) 73
Nathan Halley (15) 74
Jayden Smith (11) 75
Iwan Ellis Logan (13) 76
Jarrad Hippsley (15) 77
Sam Budding (12) 78
Corey Jones (13) 79
Caelan Hames (15) 80
Aaron Sparrow (14) 81
Amelia Phillips (12) 82
Daffydd Walters (14) 83
Tyson Wicks (13) 84
Luke Amos (12) 85
Evie Jarrett (12) 86
Jack Davies (13) 87
Jade Stammers (12) 88
Tia Rhianne Sandhu (15) 89
Alex Jones (14) 90
Gracie-May Owen 91
Isabelle Jones (11) 92
Alexander Morgan (12) 93
Ruby Tyler (12) 94
Aaliyah Morris (12) 95
Cameron Cresswell (12) 96
Joseph Jones 97
Zach Siddley (11) 98
Katie Toghill (12) 99
Joshua Morgan (11) 100
Phoebe Sizer-Hancock (12) 101
Hudson Griffiths (11) 102
Ellie Louise Thomas 103
Liberty Hetherington (12) 104
Summer Williams (13) 105
Jacob Catlow (12) 106
Charlotte Flaherty (12) 107
Ella Moseley (14) 108
Lucy Wright (11) 109
Dylan Brown (14) 110
Rosie Blinkhorn (12) 111
Mika-Leigh Ashley-Marsh 112
Jake Glover (13) 113
Dylan Draper (13) 114
Isabelle Jacklin (11) 115
Emma Lacey (12) 116
Tristan Skelton (15) 117
Macy Lyla Burns (11) 118
Rebekah Williams (15) 119
Erin Jones (13) 120
Catrin Howells (12) 121
Grace Driscoll (12) 122
Jay Bishop (13) 123
Carys Crellin (13) 124
Lewis Jones (14) 125
Tylor Sweet (11) 126
Iestyn Donovan (12) 127
Bethany Shepherd (12) 128
Phoebe Phillips (11) 129
Chloe Toop (11) 130
Amy Lee Smith (11) 131
Lauren Jex (11) 132
Ashton Bow (11) 133
Thiago Lima Westwood (14) 134
Evie Manning (12) 135
Carwyn Evans (13) 136
Thea Lloyd (12) 137
Abigail Chidgey (13) 138
Seren Sanderson (12) 139
Gracie Williams (12) 140

Ava-Lucia Warren (11) 141
Ella Jones (11) 142
Thomas Walters (13) 143
Libby Johns (13) 144
Freddie Rickards (12) 145
Anja Bennett (11) 146
Lauren Davies (13) 147
Lincoln Hall (12) 148
Madison Shellard (11) 149
Emmy Serpell (12) 150

Stoke College, Stoke By Clare

William Morris 151
Kieran Vickers 152
Alfie Cameron (13) 153

The Astley Cooper School, Hemel Hempstead

Ellis Joseph Blake (13) 154
Sarita Silwal (13) 155
Jessica Lyn Waite (14) 156
Samantha-Jane Price (11) 157
Hyed Haq (11) 158
Jamie Buckingham (12) 159
Amelia Edwards (14) 160
Sean Hayes (12) 161

Thomas Deacon Academy, Peterborough

Amel Djoudi (13) 162
Afrida Nahar (12) 163
Halwest Aziz (12) 164
Alex Turlakov (11) 165
Muhammed Junaid Malik (11) 166
Eloise Dobbing (12) 167
Aisha Ahmed (15) 168
Emilija Jovkovska (11) 169
Shniya Marie Kelly (11) 170
Arwa Jahangir (13) 171
Noor Ramzan (11) 172
Jacob Danaher (13) 173
Wiktoria Apakitsa (13) 174
Alice Lyall (12) 175
Juweria Alam (12) 176
Skaiste Sinusaite (12) 177
Leon Martin Jordan Cartledge (11) 178
Romeesa Raza (12) 179
Owais Gaibee (11) 180
Adam Cunnington (13) 181
Mahnoor Malik (12) 182
Thea Richmond (11) 183
Anwar Ali (12) 184
Maryam Iraj Yaseen (11) 185

THE STORIES

The Night At The Abandoned Building

The sirens wailed, the clouds dimmed and the weather changed after a horrific night at the abandoned building. Some people were murdered as we were messing around with dark spirit boards. I was feeling petrified. My heart was going so fast, it was hard to breathe. All that I thought about was what had happened tonight and why someone got stabbed and shot about 100 times. Why was this happening? I started to walk towards a town to tell an adult what had happened but I kept searching and there was nobody to be found at all.

Liam Bray (13)
Bishopton Centre, Billingham

The Nightmare

I had twenty-four hours to live. The second the zombie bit me I started to run to my family to tell them and say my goodbyes. I was rugby tackled and a black sack was put over my head. I felt nauseous and could barely breathe. I almost passed out. As I woke up, I was in a small room with a large spotlight pointing at me. There were three men with knives, buckets of water and guns. I started to shout out loud for help but then, all of a sudden, I awoke somewhere I couldn't even imagine.

Ryan Robert Briggs (13)
Bishopton Centre, Billingham

The Betrayal

Tonight is when everything ends. Tonight, the Dark Archer puts his plan into action; I have only twelve hours or millions will die. It's not safe. Pushing the door open, the bloody body lies on the floor; the Dark Archer's standing over it. He has killed another innocent person. Enough! "The end is near," he growls. Quickly, his arrow flies towards me. He runs and I chase. My heart is racing. Then, he appears behind me. Suddenly, I am being hunted. I become the prey. Am I going to fail my city? As he reveals his identity, I feel betrayed.

Paul Nathan Parewa (12)
Rivers Education Support Centre, Hoddesdon

The Chase

Boom! What on earth was that? Night-time covered the city like a black blanket. Police sirens could be heard for miles: a shrill wailing like someone in pain. They were coming for me but they didn't know where I was. I was excited but nervous; the thrill of the chase was like being young again, running around the playground, wanting to be caught. But, this wasn't a game! A dark alley with its spooky shadows was a welcome escape. It was damp and the stench of filfthy, rotten food made me want to vomit. *Boom!* What on earth was that?

Charlie Curtis (14)
Rivers Education Support Centre, Hoddesdon

The Hunter Becomes Hunted

They were coming! Darkness fell like ash from a cigarette. I could see them now; the hunter had become the hunted. My bag filled with the gang's bounty, every step, every breath was becoming shorter. "Stop," he yelled. They've got me, it's over! I had become the prey and in the blink of an eye, blood fell. Was it mine? No, it was his... he wailed, he screamed. Every cut became deeper, soaking down my shirt, but he was holding on - he wasn't ready to die, he was only fourteen. He was my friend. I had let him down.

Divine Ephraim (14)
Rivers Education Support Centre, Hoddesdon

Unexpected

All I could see from left to right were beautiful beach huts and friendly families. Everybody seemed to think that I was an alien. I was being looked up and down by people I'd never seen before. I was scared, I felt out of place. I looked down at my phone: *I'm here!* This really wasn't what I expected. My heart froze, my stomach turned and my brain stopped. It was him. I tried to run but my legs wouldn't move. *Bang!* One shot. My own best friend holding the gun. It was over. So unexpected!

Lennon Pearse (13)
Rivers Education Support Centre, Hoddesdon

Hunting

Ten. Their scent was intoxicating. I observed them from afar, my inhuman mind going over the many brutal ways I could make them shriek and beg for their ignominious existence. *Nine*. The moon's bright rays of hope were dimmed by the clouds, taking away their only source of hope and sanity. *Eight... Seven*. The wind picked up, bringing wails and screams that played in my bed like music. *Six... Five*. All became silent, bringing peace to the land for those few hopeful seconds. *Four*. "Run for your lives..." A bone-chilling roar broke the eerie stillness. *Three... Two... One*.

Sarah Bissaker
Shire Oak Academy, Walsall Wood

Wanted

Exhausted, isolated and petrified, I struck my last match, a brief intermission of illumination pierced the darkness. I knew there was little time, little time before I'd be caught, little time before I'd be punished. I took a deep breath, swallowing all panic-struck thoughts... then exhaled. I became alert to a muffled noise in the distance. Sliding down the ravine, heart-pounding frantically, I covered myself with leaves. Sweat streamed down my face, pooling in the socket of my eye. I could hear them getting closer, panting dogs sniffing me out. How long would I last before I was caught?

Grace Simmons
Shire Oak Academy, Walsall Wood

The Hunter

I'm a survivor, a hunter. I hear my pulse. The steady thrumming is an almost comfort faced with what I'm about to do. Adrenaline levels rising. Every nerve on edge. Every brain cell screaming at me to stop. *Stop!* I'm in too far now. I could turn and walk away, run away... but I'd be running forever. This suffering would never cease. So, here I am, about to put a bullet through the brain of the first person who successfully cured cancer. This secret can't get out. They walk past, unseeing, unknowing. One bullet... I'm a hunter; a survivor. Always, forever...

Daisy Reynolds (12)
Shire Oak Academy, Walsall Wood

Sleep Paralysis

Trapped. I'm trapped in an endless abyss. There's only nothingness. Darkness engulfs me. Anxiety consumes me. My own temptation compels me to ruin myself further until I have been consumed by it utterly. I'm numb, numb to the pain of being solitary. Although I'm alone, I can't help but think that someone or something is with me. It has complete and utter power over my being, my life, my future. Someone omniscient and omnipresent rules over me. I'm unknowing to the power of which it possesses. What could it be that reigns over me as I lie, frightened and feeble?

Kat Zachariou
Shire Oak Academy, Walsall Wood

Hide-And-Seek

Twenty-four hours to hide but nowhere to run. I need to run, need to hide but how? I'm prey getting stalked by a predator. Eyes seem to follow my every move through cracks. Hide. I'm in a small hospital locker, trying to hide from my stalker. Time to go, I've been spotted. Running through the hospital, I have to find the right place. Tripping, I fall. I can't escape this living nightmare.
I am woken up by the sound of thunder. *Where am I? What is that?* There is a skeletal figure in front of me. It is half-human, half-skeleton... Evie!

Alexandra Peat (13)
Shire Oak Academy, Walsall Wood

Forever Running

The alarm sounded... run! Thirty minutes to get to a safer place. Where that was, I didn't know. I had no idea. I had to keep running. Never stopping. Not for them. Not for anyone. We were running for survival. Forever running. The second alarm rang out across the fields and cities. They were out, on their way. People have probably already been hunted but I couldn't stop to help. I couldn't stop. Not for food. Not for water. Not for rest. Not for anything. Not now they were coming. Faster... Faster... Gaining speed... Closer... Or so I thought.

Ruby May Howell (13)
Shire Oak Academy, Walsall Wood

The Hunt

I clutched my head in sudden agony as I experienced hazy hallucinations mocking me. It was every man for himself. I heard a profound cacophony of blood-curdling screams as I bolted around the corner; I couldn't leave them. Sirens encapsulated the dusty, eerie and dilapidated avenue. I tasted blood on my lips and felt sweat rise around my collarbones. I heard the cavernous thump of the sirens getting closer and closer as trepidation choked me. I contemplated my choices, should I save myself from being hunted or should I be the cruel and wretched hunter?

Iman Sajjad Bhatti (11)
Shire Oak Academy, Walsall Wood

Where Are You?

I can't run for much longer. I've been running for hours. Maybe it's gone but maybe it's still behind me. It has to be here somewhere. My stomach is swirling as I race flat out through the spine-chilling, deserted forest. *Wake up!* That's all I want to do but this is not a dream, it is a nightmare! *Crunch.* I feel my heart surge. I look behind me but I can't see anything except complete darkness. The noise gets louder and louder. I know it's behind me. I know what's going to happen. I know it's the end.

Emma Feilden (13)
Shire Oak Academy, Walsall Wood

Hide-And-Seek

The seekers were close, marching closer to find us. *Stomp!* They were right next to us. We ran until we couldn't breathe but we just carried on running. I saw a dangerous cave and hid there until dark. Dark fell, consuming all of the city. I ran until my legs couldn't carry me anymore. It was there, looking down at me. "Come with me, now!" the thing shouted at me. I got up and followed it until I made a run for it. I slipped, injuring myself.
"My leg!" I shouted. It heard. It charged straight at me. *No!*

Eric Hikins (12)
Shire Oak Academy, Walsall Wood

Hunted

"Go, drive, go!" Sirens blaring behind me, the screech of the wheels on the road slice painfully through my head. My heart pounds through my chest trying to escape. They'll lock me up and throw the key away for all the terrible damage I have caused during this riot. Nothing. I'll have nothing left, even if I do get released in the end. I may look selfish but I can't stop now. I must push on! Lights grow brighter and brighter behind me, growing closer and closer towards me. Adrenaline gushes throughout me. This is the end. Hunted.

Nicole Nayler (12)
Shire Oak Academy, Walsall Wood

The Hunted

"I'm the one to do the killing," whispering to himself, Wesley spoke.
Wesley was known to be the most fierce and painstaking warrior in all of the six dimensions. Wesley was hunting for the Lady of Conan in the third dimension, when he was told by some very suspicious locals that there had been a sighting in the hills of a lady that fitted the description, going by the name of Martha Bennet. Wesley decided that he'd check the area out and got himself in a pickle. There she was, on fire, using her full power to defeat the man.

Harvey Bird
Shire Oak Academy, Walsall Wood

Reuse Panthera Leo

The briefing was done, the flight was over. Zach had arrived. He was at the Kiyozom Toji, the temple where the beast settled many, many years ago. Zach's mission was to execute this mutant creature and he had to complete it solo! He was at the temple now, preparing to venture inside. Myths of the monstrosity Zach was hunting down had been around for years but the Reuse Panthera Leo wasn't a myth at all. Zach had all the gear he needed to accomplish his mission. His P11 locked and loaded. Now, after years of training, the hunt was on!

Josh Turner
Shire Oak Academy, Walsall Wood

Tunnel Of Terror!

There I was, hiding, surrounded by darkness. My heart was beating faster than ever. It was like a game of hide-and-seek, a life or death situation. Lost children screamed for their parents as *it* was about to be unleashed. All of a sudden, a loud roar echoed through the tunnel. Could this be my final breath? *It* slowly came closer and closer to me and its footsteps got louder and louder. I clutched my knees and hoped that I would wake up and it would just be a dream but when I opened my eyes, *it* was approaching me...

Zak Moulick (12)
Shire Oak Academy, Walsall Wood

Hunted

We had four hours to escape before they came, and if we didn't, it was game over. Trapped inside a long maze in the dead of night, not knowing what was around the corner. The maze was filled with deathly traps. Not everyone would survive. *Bang!* The sound of a gun echoed. Someone was there. *Bang!* There it was again. A shadow came around the corner, a long, shiny gun aimed at our faces. Our hearts were pounding, all we could do was run, but there was not much chance that we would survive. *Bang!* We ran for it...

Ava Webb (11)
Shire Oak Academy, Walsall Wood

Disasters Destroy

The houses collapsed. The people cried. They ran as fast as they could. It had happened again. Why us? The bricks from the houses covered the floor, we were trapped. Blood covered the entire pavement. The water had come quicker than expected. We had to swim. But to where? We had nowhere to go. No place to live. It was important to live a normal life here. We had constantly feared something like this would happen again. But, we had no money to move away from it. We tried to take extreme precautions but nothing ever worked. We were trapped.

Abby Gray
Shire Oak Academy, Walsall Wood

The Hunted

This all started on a Thursday night when Evon, Jason and I all went out to meet our other friends. The time was 10:33pm. We met there to visit our friend's grave. We always met there to remember him. As we were gathered there, a man came running out towards us saying, "I killed your friend, you're next!" All five of us ran, trying to find the exit. Finally, we were all out and sighed with relief. The same night, we went back to Evon's to talk. *Knock knock*, the door went.
"Hide!" I screamed.

Chelsie Cox (13)
Shire Oak Academy, Walsall Wood

The Chase

Flashing blue lights illuminated the sky. Sirens resonated through the atmosphere. They were gaining on us, we had to act fast. Dog, our driver, skirted left. We then took a sharp right. We had hit the jackpot, 20,000,000 dollars. We could not lose it now, after all this hard grafting. The police had one objective and that was to take us out. Getting closer and closer, they rammed the back of our motor. However, were approached the bypass. It was now or never. We drifted into the old sewer. We thought we were alone. But, we were wrong.

Bradley Green (15)
Shire Oak Academy, Walsall Wood

Hungry, Thirsty And Trying To Survive

Hungry, thirsty, I staggered on, reluctant to go back, unwilling to look back. Minutes had gone past, maybe even seconds, since the breakout. Only God could help me now. I could hear the sirens, the most hated noise in the entire world. I knew it was up to me. "Who are you?" a young girl innocently asked, clearly not knowing the truth.
"I-I-I thought I would come up for a stroll," I stuttered, clearly not thinking it through properly. Little did she know what I would have to do. I had no choice. She had to go.

Alexander Andrew Walker (12)
Shire Oak Academy, Walsall Wood

The Hunted

I still have nightmares about it, when they came after us. I can remember it like it was yesterday. I remember when we were at the graveyard, looking at my mum's grave. When we turned around, that's when it all started. All the dead people crawled from their graves. We were scared. There was only one thing we could do. That was to run. They followed. We were running for our lives. When we noticed they were going away, we stopped and noticed a bunker. We've been here for three months now. We can only go out during daylight.

Charlie Hems
Shire Oak Academy, Walsall Wood

Hunted

The hunt was on... sirens started to get closer towards me. I ran onto the main road, I went to cross over; hazard lights were going off. I was so panicked. I looked behind me and there was a man walking closer. I saw him and started to run. I tried to speed up but tried not to make it look obvious. "Argh," I screamed. Flashing lights had turned fluorescent orange like a flame. My phone had almost died and I couldn't make contact with anyone... *Bang!* He grabbed hold of me and pushed me. "Help! Quick!"

Amelia-Rose Price (13)
Shire Oak Academy, Walsall Wood

Operation Bite Mark

We were travelling to the place, the place that promised to make everything better when we heard the sirens screeching around us. They were coming. Nothing to stop them, no chance to outrun them. We tried our best but they were too strong. Never stopping, never breathing but always hungry for more. We didn't know what we were doing. They told us it would be fine, that it was safe but we had no options now: no government, no trust, no friends. It was just the apocalypse and there it was, leering over us. I was absolutely done for.

Campbell Smith (11)
Shire Oak Academy, Walsall Wood

The Hunt

The hunt... it'd started. The siren wailed and everybody ran in different directions towards the maze. My group of friends and I ran to the same part of the maze, some kind of small passage. There was something we were all looking for: a safe place at the end of the maze. I was wondering when the sirens would go off again. Should I be wondering when that... thing... would come to murder us? Sirens suddenly started to wail again. The enormous doors heaved open letting *it* come out for us. We were officially being hunted.

Kylan Bullock (11)
Shire Oak Academy, Walsall Wood

The Hunters

It hadn't been long since the incident. My sister, gone with those... monsters. You may think that zombies and vampires are fake, but have you heard of a hunter? I didn't think so. They have both an urge for brains like a zombie and are careless like a vampire. The woods were full of the stench of rotting. I couldn't help but think about how my sister was gone. They were monsters, murderers. I heard the cries of her in agony. I was there. I felt teeth on me. They'd got me. I had been hunted. See you soon, Melody...

Aleesha Scarlet Barrier (11)
Shire Oak Academy, Walsall Wood

Hunted

The hunt was on. It was like hide-and-seek but death or life. I could hear the sirens, the screeching. I could hear the zombies coming for me. I was stuck in the maze, the maze with nothing but twists and turns. I knew there was no escape, no mercy. I was counting the seconds I had left. One hundred, ninety-nine... They were getting closer by the second. The maze bushes were moving. Sixty-five, sixty-four, sixty-three. It got me by the ankles. I fell to the ground. It was dragging me into the bush. There were two seconds left...

Paige Dunning (13)
Shire Oak Academy, Walsall Wood

Hide-And-Seek

Clang! I was hiding in the basement. I didn't know what I was hiding from but I knew it wasn't friendly. I could hear it coming down the stairs. What could I do? It was saying something, "Don't hide, I'm friendly." I knew it was lying. My heart was beating out of my chest. Soon after, I heard a big bang upstairs. This was my chance to get out of this house. As I tiptoed out of the house, there was a siren I didn't recognise. Wait, could it be? It was. WWII had started. Oh no, I was stuck...

Mai Jones
Shire Oak Academy, Walsall Wood

Run For Your Life Or Else!

They were there, behind me. I was sure of it. Their feet pounding with every step they took along the dry, cracked earth, viciously telling me to stop or there would be trouble. Reluctantly, I carried on until I came to a halt. There was something in front of me standing with great posture. It stared at me, its pale, moonlight eyes baring into my soul. I suddenly realised that it was a wolf but not any wolf, there was something odd about it. Maybe it was even trying to tell me something. Then I realised: I was being hunted...

Yvie Mae Bowler (12)
Shire Oak Academy, Walsall Wood

The Natural Disaster

I had only twenty-four hours to get out of the city. The forecast had a warning that there was going to be a tsunami. That meant the city would be destroyed by the horrible wave that would come. Twenty-four hours later, the tsunami hit the city and destroyed every building and thing in sight.
Now, we are in Florida with a new house and new jobs which give us loads of money which helps us to get furniture. But, there was bad news back in the city. Some people didn't make it to the flight, meaning lots of people died.

Connor Ray Lemord (13)
Shire Oak Academy, Walsall Wood

The Key

The light flickers. I don't know where I'm going, but I know I need to find it. The key is my only escape from the huntsman. But, where is it? Room after room, hour after hour, it's like a game of hide-and-seek. I hear alarms being set off. Is that him? *Thud. Thud. Thud.* I hear his footsteps. My legs are taking my body somewhere but I don't know where. I see a key but I think he's got me. My lips are trembling, my legs are stuck and I can't breathe. No one can get away from the hunter.

Ruby Grace Walklate (12)
Shire Oak Academy, Walsall Wood

Infection

My heart raced. Thoughts resonated through my head. *Would I make it?* I was the last one. They were vultures seeking me. I pinched myself to check if I was just daydreaming, but this was no dream. It was anything but. The virus took over their innocent minds and transformed them into senseless creatures. The worst part was that I used to be friends with them; the virus took that away as well. I decided to run, run as far as I could. But, it was no use. I dashed for the next corridor but my time was cut short.

Lucy Heeley
Shire Oak Academy, Walsall Wood

Hunted

There I was, I could hear the deafening shouting behind me. They were chasing me, hunting me. But why? What did I do? Well, I'd figure it out soon enough when they finally caught me. The ominous light reflected off the moon that was shining down on me as I ran through the filthy alleyway. As much as I wanted to, I couldn't stop, not if I wanted to survive. A million thoughts roamed around my head; my family, my friends, my job. It was all just a mess. I figured I would pay for something I didn't even do.

Jack Clarke (11)
Shire Oak Academy, Walsall Wood

Hunted Story

A flashing light comes in and out of visibility; this is it. This is not a drill; this is survival! For many, this is just an idea. For me, it is a cruel reality. This is a program to fight overpopulation and calm down the rising crime rates; a scheme so the rich get richer and the poor get poorer, fuelled by the greed of government officials. Every person is in on it but not everyone will come out alive. No rules, no restrictions and no mercy. Every minute feels like hours and is so intense. I'm being hunted!

Harry Ttiniozou
Shire Oak Academy, Walsall Wood

The Werewolf

This heart-racing chase has been going on for what feels like hours. I catch my breath against one of the long, tall trees, just waiting to be pounced on by death. I slither around the tree to see the creature, staring me down with such hunger. It has razor-sharp fangs and on the side of its mouth is drool dripping down onto the floor. Instantly, the beast darts at me with all its might. Adrenaline rushes to my body, my heart pounces and my legs bolt towards the distance as I try to escape from the hairy monster.

Yazmin Tolley
Shire Oak Academy, Walsall Wood

Being Hunted

It was late, the moon painted the sky with a faint white light and I was sneaking through a large scale of tall bushes that seemed to never end. I was so cold. I couldn't find a way out. For an unknown reason, I would discover an exit but every time it approached, it would always slam shut before I got close enough to escape. I didn't know why. I finally found one more exit, but this time it didn't shut. I had a slight bit of hope until... these ear-piercing sirens wailed, loudly. I was being hunted.

Mollie Taylor
Shire Oak Academy, Walsall Wood

Hide-And-Seek

I walk down the street, the bloodstained road brings tears to my eyes. I still have nightmares about that day. When I think about it, I can hear my heartbeat through my chest. How he walked past me, how I thought I would never see my family again and they would never see me! I have vowed never to call him by his name. Now, it is always *he*. The vivid image of him strolling down the stairs, the gun in his hand. But, at that time, I didn't know that that very gun would end my whole family's life.

Emily Brabbin
Shire Oak Academy, Walsall Wood

The Hunt

Suddenly, the pressure was on... There were howls of pain and fear. Sirens wailed through the weary streets. Chased and wanted, I ran all I could. Would this be a dead end to my plan? Sirens got closer and closer. The prison wasn't my home. I needed a way out. Right there, a huge, faded, black entrance... Was this my way out of this terrible mess? The thump of my heart pounding rapidly, I bolted my way through. Would I ever escape from this wretched tangle or would I be stuck in a prison cell forever?

Varia Daro Aziz (12)
Shire Oak Academy, Walsall Wood

Hunted By Something Impossible

The doors opened and with a loud growl, a face appeared. It looked like a dog but much larger. It pounced towards me but banged its head on a solid wall of glass. I knew that I didn't have much time before I was... hunted. I ran as fast as I could, wasting energy as I went, slowly down, becoming more and more fatigued. I needed rest but if I stopped, it would catch up. Down a pitch-black hallway, into a pitch-black room, the monster's red eyes stared at me, its teeth showing. I was about to die.

Ethan Clarke (12)
Shire Oak Academy, Walsall Wood

Break Time

We had to run now. They were onto us. We scattered out of sight of them, I got away with most of it but Tim still had some. *Bang!* What was that? Nevertheless, I staggered on. Where would I end up next? *Wah! Wah! Wah!* The siren still rang in my ears from earlier. What did I do now? I'd been running non-stop trying to do this and had no other men. I didn't know where the police were. This was worse than torture! Hold on, maybe there was a way. The police could become the hunted!

Olly Foster
Shire Oak Academy, Walsall Wood

The Forest

One stormy night down in the deep, dark woods, a mysterious, timid man roamed the forest. Jumping at any sight or noise, the whistle of the wind and all the other strange noises started to frighten the man. The legend once said that people who went in the dark depths of the gloomy forest, never came back. People believed that there was a monster that lived in a cage and the only thing it ate was people.
All of a sudden, there was a noise. He turned around. There was nothing until, *bang!*

Eloise Peach
Shire Oak Academy, Walsall Wood

The Chase

I couldn't go on for much longer... I ran and ran but my legs began to collapse. I knew the forest well, I could get away from them. They thought I was a bad person. I... I didn't mean to. As I ran, I couldn't get the image out of my mind. My legs sagged to the floor like jelly. I couldn't go on... I just... gave up. I heard the sirens all around, getting closer and closer. This was the end, they were going to get me. I wished I could fight, try to convince them. Help me... please...

Millie Spruce (13)
Shire Oak Academy, Walsall Wood

Prison Break

The sirens wailed, the racing cars catching up every second, every minute. I jumped into a bush, a spiky bush that hurt. The cars drove past. I held my breath so they couldn't hear my screams. Once the cars disappeared down the road, I got out of the bush and ran in the opposite direction. Some people would call this a prison break. I'd been sentenced to thirty-five years for something that I didn't do. I supposedly robbed the biggest bank in America, but it was a dirty lookalike of me!

Zak Charles Carley (11)
Shire Oak Academy, Walsall Wood

The Hunted Silhouette Of A Figure

It strolled slowly with no intention other than to puncture its prey's skin. It waited. It waited longer. Then, it came to its senses to pounce and it attacked its prey, slicing it with its pointed fangs. Then it vanished. It was gone. That was the end, surely? But it wasn't. It was gone for now. I walked off in shock but there it was, standing there. The figure. So I sprinted off but there it was again and again, it was everywhere. It snarled at me. It jumped at me. Luckily, I woke up!

Christopher Pedley (13)
Shire Oak Academy, Walsall Wood

Hide-And-Seek

There was nothing but gunshots. The hunt had begun. I ran into the night thinking I wasn't being followed but I was wrong. Three dark, black figures from the unknown were coming towards me. I was struck with panic and froze on the spot. They caught me. With a roar of flames, they cuffed my hands and dragged me back to where I first was - the maze of doom. I went deep into the maze and hid. I was found. The figure looked me in the eye and pointed a gun at my face. Total darkness. I was dead.

Isla McCullagh
Shire Oak Academy, Walsall Wood

The Box

As I slowly came to my senses, I realised three things: I was in a box. Rising. Fast. I slowly stood up and looked around me. There was nothing. With a sudden thud, the box stopped. Two mechanical doors opened and I walked out into a somewhat large room. On a chair at the side of me was a note: 'First test'. Suddenly, three different creatures came at me. They were wearing rags. I ran out of the gate at the far end of the room. I knew one thing: I was not the hunter, I was the hunted.

Mayson Joynes (13)
Shire Oak Academy, Walsall Wood

My Last Hours

The hourglass was almost empty. I had to get out... somehow. There must be another exit. I looked up in fear, trying to find a way out of the damp, old shed. I saw a small steamed window. Tearing up, I came to the realisation that I was not going to be leaving this shack alive. I slowly glanced over towards the hourglass, it was completely empty. I felt my heart stop for a second and a giant lump came to my throat as the door that was locked, slammed open. This was the end. This was the end.

Maisie Elizabeth Andrews (16)
Shire Oak Academy, Walsall Wood

The Hunt Is On

I thought they would never find me, but they did. It was just an ordinary night. I was sitting on my bed playing on my phone. Then, I got a phone call from an unspecified person. I answered the phone, not knowing who it was or what would happen. It was at that moment that I heard sirens and slams. I ran out of my bedroom, tried to open the front door but it seemed stuck. Then, I tried the back door but that was stuck too! Suddenly, a man slammed down the door holding a bloody murder weapon!

KJ Parton
Shire Oak Academy, Walsall Wood

Hunted

I heard heavy footsteps coming towards me. Could it be a werewolf? I trembled in fear as the wood was well known for its vicious, flesh-eating werewolves. There was a lot of well-known attacks. If a kid was gone, not long after they would be found dead in the wood. I heard the faint sound of sniffing. I had to get out of there and fast. I heard police sirens. I started to run to the sirens. Suddenly, I felt a tight grip on my arm, then a pull. *I need to get out of here*, I thought.

Eva Webster
Shire Oak Academy, Walsall Wood

The Hunt (Natural Disaster)

I couldn't run for much longer. I was tired, upset and stressed. I was confused. I wanted to know where my mom and dad were but I couldn't find them. I was scared. I was in a field lying down on my own. I had just been in a tornado. Everyone around me was gone. It was ruined. I started to get up and I looked around, people's bodies were not nice. I started to run because I didn't want to see it again. I wanted this to all just go away so I just kept on running and running.

Olivia Sturch
Shire Oak Academy, Walsall Wood

Hunted

My life was a misery since my little sister was murdered. It made me want to find the soul who was responsible. It was a night I would never forget. A night of horror as we were left alone for just an hour when I heard an ear-piercing shriek. I ran into her room and there was blood everywhere, my sister gone. My parents got home to find me on the floor with her favourite dress in my hand and the pale, bloody corpse of my little sister. I was the main suspect. Everyone thought it was me.

Lydia Scott
Shire Oak Academy, Walsall Wood

Hunted

The ear-piercing siren went off and at that exact moment, I knew the hunt was on. The predator was far behind but I knew I couldn't stop running, not until I was far away. As I ran as fast as I could, I heard leaves ruffling. At that point, I knew there wasn't just one animal chasing me, there were many. I needed to find out what was chasing me and how many there were. As I looked up, I could see a gate. I realised that all I needed to do to be safe was get over that gate...

Molly Ivins (12)
Shire Oak Academy, Walsall Wood

Zombie Hunted

I couldn't run for much longer. I was running away from these zombies. It wasn't safe. They knew where I lived. We were close to the end of the road. It had to be here somewhere, the car that could get me away. I reached the car and I yelled that we had to leave now. There were sirens screaming next to me and I was confused. I had twenty-four hours to get away from them.
Now, when I have to go to sleep, I still have nightmares about it and it's really frightening.

Paige Startup
Shire Oak Academy, Walsall Wood

Vampire Outbreak

I ran so fast. I wasn't aware of how fast I was running but I had to carry on before he caught me. I thought I wasn't going to get caught... All I had was until the dawn to get away. I could sense him in all directions, he wasn't going to stop until he caught me. It was like cat and mouse. He was a vampire and I was a helpless thirteen-year-old girl. I did a stupid thing, leaving the house at night. I should've listened to my big brother when he told me about them.

Alicia Heath
Shire Oak Academy, Walsall Wood

The Hunt Begins

I was stuck, stuck in the middle of nowhere. I was lost in a graveyard. I was looking for something, something like a grave. This grave was my dad's. I loved him so much. He should not have died when he did. He did not deserve that. It should not have been him. He was only protecting me from the driver. I'd got lost running from something. *Guilt*. It should have been me. I missed him so much. He was my best friend. I felt so bad, lonely, scared and frightened.

Zoe Tolley
Shire Oak Academy, Walsall Wood

The Hunt

It was there that night. In the midst of the night, they came for me. I was lost in the tsunami of people in the streets of London. I had escaped my dreaded stepmother. I had never really been out of the house before, I was always locked away in the cupboard under the stairs with only a sleeping bag for a bed which I had brought with me. I crept under a bus stop opposite the Houses of Parliament to spend the night and then I saw them... the gunmen, hunting me down.

Kyle Luke Chambers (12)
Shire Oak Academy, Walsall Wood

The Hunt Was On!

The hunt was on. It was dark. I ran in the dark. I knew it would be soon when they caught me. I had to hide.
I wish I'd never done it. It was his fault. I wished I wasn't there. It all started on a sunny Sunday morning. He barged into my room like an idiot, so, I killed him. I didn't want to.
I had to run. My parents would have caught me if I didn't. It wouldn't be long until I heard the sirens. I knew I was going to get caught.

Callum Sedgwick
Shire Oak Academy, Walsall Wood

Nowhere To Run...

I couldn't run much longer. Suddenly, I could hear footsteps in the distance. I didn't know where to go. I ran, ran as far as I could run. I knew I only had a few minutes left, a few minutes until they found me. All of a sudden, I fell to the cold, hard ground. The footsteps were slowly getting closer and closer. I knew I had to run but I couldn't. I tried to pull myself up but I only got a little bit further until *bang!* Then I was dead.

Sophie Eloise Webb (12)
Shire Oak Academy, Walsall Wood

Disaster Has Fallen

The ground started to shake, people began to panic. My drink began to swirl around my cup and without warning, I was up and hunting for safety. On my way to safety, I saw people falling over left, right and centre. One woman was helplessly trying to get her kids away from the danger. In the distance, a man in a car wildly drove into a local building site causing the building to collapse. All of a sudden, there was a large explosion and then all was silent.

Ciaran Yates
Shire Oak Academy, Walsall Wood

The Maze

I had twenty-four hours... I was running through a maze, the walls were about 100 metres tall. All I could hear was a very loud buzzing sound. It felt like it went on forever. As I came up to an exit, there were guards. I had to get around them somehow. There was a stick on the floor. I used it to distract them. Suddenly, I was cornered, they were corning for me. I ran. I came to a dead end. I turned around. They were there. I was being hunted!

Mitchell Meeson
Shire Oak Academy, Walsall Wood

Zombie Apocalypse

We were losing hope of ever finding a cure for this disease. With no government and no army, we were never going to make it, were we? We got into the car and drove on, leaving Camp 29 behind. We drove on the highway, before arriving at the CDC (Centre for Disease Control). We got inside, it was dark and I was scared. The group started walking over to the door and it was shaking. I screamed as it crashed open - it was over. We were being hunted.

Evie Wilson (12)
Shire Oak Academy, Walsall Wood

Run!

I still have nightmares about it. I had twenty-four hours to get out before it would come after us. We had to get out now. As soon as it escaped, we would have to run. The sirens wailed. We ran, we sprinted. We were close, so close but still so far. I couldn't run for much longer. I thought it would come. I didn't know what it looked like but I imagined it to be a horrible creature. I kept running. I looked up and there it was.

Emily Jackson (14)
Shire Oak Academy, Walsall Wood

The Hunt Of The Spy!

I looted a bank. Someone called the feds. I ran out of there and jumped over the fence. I ended up on the roof of the building and the person up there was a spy. He tried to shoot me with a sleep gun. He ran and ran until I went into a massive ditch. Then I had to jump onto the ladder beside the wall. He and another spy went around the corner. He went for the shot but then I dodged it. Then the other spy jumped on top of me.

Tyler Adam Roden (13)
Shire Oak Academy, Walsall Wood

The Hunt

As I hid behind the green coat of the bark, I tried calming my breath, but it swirled out in short, shaky gasps. A snap in the distance caused a bead of sweat to trickle down my forehead. Like a ghost, I turned silently on my perch. Chestnut-brown fur covered the magnificent beast and mahogany horns protruded from its head. Soundlessly, I drew my bow, slug the arrow and pulled back the cord. *Thwang!* At the speed of light, the steel-tipped arrow embedded in the fur and the animal roared with pain.

Samuel Vincent (12)
St Cuthbert's Catholic High School, Newcastle Upon Tyne

Could I Make It?

I had thirty minutes to reach the border, there was no time to waste. Time was ticking second by precious second, every breath I took was valuable as it may have been my last. I couldn't run for much longer, they would hear me. Minutes passed by, I could hear engines zooming past me and muffled voices appearing from the distance. This was what my life had come to, this dismal world with the end always in sight. As the border crept towards me, a man was waiting. Could I make it in time?

Ashtone Noel Hindes (12)
St Cuthbert's Catholic High School, Newcastle Upon Tyne

The Chase

I had become the prey. I felt like a hyena being chased by a lion. The sky was black and the sticks on the ground were another obstacle I had to overcome. My adrenaline was pumping, my legs were aching and my rapidly beating heart felt like it could explode from my chest. I'd never run faster in my life. I started to feel my aching legs slow down with exhaustion and I could hear the sirens coming closer and closer towards me. I tripped...

Hussain Jabar (13)
St Cuthbert's Catholic High School, Newcastle Upon Tyne

The Hunt

The sirens started. They would find me soon, I needed to find somewhere to hide for the night. I could go to my parents' house, but I didn't remember them... I didn't remember anything. I didn't even remember coming to this place, all I remember was life in hell. Everything went blurry - the blue and red sirens were all I could see, the only thing that stood out to me. That was when I found out where I really was.

James Dann (12)
St Cuthbert's Catholic High School, Newcastle Upon Tyne

The Hunt

I could not run for much longer. Every inhalation felt like a needle stabbing down my throat. I had a feeling that my rusty legs would give up on me. It was like the marathon I ran back in the day - before they captured me. There wasn't time to think of that, not now. The moon was ghostly, watching me from above. My leather boots sunk into the mud as I dashed through the forest. All of a sudden, I heard a siren wailing and saw the lights looming over me. I knew this was the end.

Hasib Younis
St Cuthbert's Catholic High School, Newcastle Upon Tyne

The Prey

Today my life changed forever, I was completely lost in a large forest. I knew that I wasn't going to survive for long. The clouds started to turn to eerie darkness. I had to find something now. Suddenly, I saw some branches - I remembered I had the lighter. Finally, I could warm myself... I heard someone near me. I looked to the very corner of my eye; there was nothing. It was too late, I had become the prey.

Phillipe Coloma
St Cuthbert's Catholic High School, Newcastle Upon Tyne

The Endless Run

Running, legs aching and dehydrated, I wanted to stop. I wanted to stop but I couldn't, knowing that if I did, that would be the last I saw of this decaying world. I tried to put distance between them, however when I thought they were gone, they came swarming back, devouring anything alive and transforming them into vile, mindless entities! This once beautiful and tranquil world changed from some unnecessary experiments into something foreign and unknown to everyone! People changed, civilisation gone to dust and turmoil. If you see something walking in the middle of the road bumbling about, run!

Zachary Phillips-Sinigoj (12)
St John Baptist CIW High School, Aberdare

Life Is Hunted

One day, my life was destroyed. Before that, my life was great. My life was destroyed by Nan. She said that my father had died. He'd committed suicide. I knew that the funeral was looming. Suddenly, the funeral came. We had my father's favourite song 'Every Breath You Take'. The funeral came to an end. Rapidly, the bell rang at my house. It was the police! I said, "Come in."
They said, "Your father's grave was destroyed last night."
The next day, I hunted for the person that destroyed my father's grave. It wasn't my fault that I killed them.

Nathan Halley (15)
St John Baptist CIW High School, Aberdare

The FBI Hunt

It was just a normal day at home. *Bang! Bang!* "It's the FBI, open up!" Oh no, I've got to run. *Bang!* They knocked down the door. I jumped out of the window and ran as fast as I could through the forest, trying to dodge every tree. "He went over there, get him." I hid behind a tree. I was scared. Oh no. It was an FBI agent. "I'm going to get you out of this mess."
"Thank you, Sir."
"Don't mention it. Look, so here's the plan. I will... arrest you. Ha ha! I've got you now!"
"No!"

Jayden Smith (11)
St John Baptist CIW High School, Aberdare

It Came From The Depths Of The Storm

Searching, I trudged through swampy sewage water. It'd been days since the tornadoes and floods ravished any signs of human civilisation. Few of us survived, those who did retreated to the sewers, taking shelter from the forces of nature wreaking havoc on the surface. It was safe in the underbelly of our once great city, or so we thought...
As I rejoined the remaining population, I saw something scuttle in the background, a sinister silhouette sneaking, but before I could take a breath, it struck. Surviving citizens were taken one by one. We realised we were being hunted...

Iwan Ellis Logan (13)
St John Baptist CIW High School, Aberdare

Behind Me!

Crunch! Steadily walking through the bizarre, unknown forest, walking consciously and slowly, I didn't know where to adventure too. I noticed one tree that was rotten and looked dead. Suddenly, I heard a rattling noise from behind me. Taking a big gulp nervously, adrenaline shot my nerves. Butterflies in my stomach were turning into eagles and goosebumps appeared like mountains on my hand. As I was about to turn around, heavy rain filled the sky and lashed down like drapery. Should I turn around and face whatever was behind me? Another noise appeared so I decided to run...

Jarrad Hippsley (15)
St John Baptist CIW High School, Aberdare

The Escape

I'd got thirty minutes to the border when a bullet whirred through the trees. We hurried to a ditch and waited.
"We're not safe," said a person beside me.
"Don't lose hope," I whispered.
Over a loud microphone, a voice yelled, "Prisoner 592Y7 and 592Y7, come out!"
We had similar names and that's how we became friends.
I replied, "You slaughtered all our friends!"
Then suddenly, we heard soldiers coming from a large base, marching towards us. We had nowhere to go except up in the trees. In the trees, a light came from a distance, approaching us...

Sam Budding (12)
St John Baptist CIW High School, Aberdare

Hunted

Where could I hide? They were after me! My leg was bleeding, my clothes were battered and my shotgun was out of ammo. Suddenly, a battered and infected hand smashed through the windscreen of the Jeep I was hiding behind. "They're here!" I muttered. "The infected!"
Without hesitation, I wrenched open the Jeep's door and started the engine. The hand now revealed an infected human. I reversed into it and cut the corner. I could see the way out, when suddenly the Jeep hit the curb and toppled. I was preparing to get eaten when suddenly, they dropped down dead...

Corey Jones (13)
St John Baptist CIW High School, Aberdare

Forest Of Sorrow

I heard rustling in the bushes, thus my ears pricked up.
Suddenly, I sprang to my feet and was on the run.
Adrenaline coursed through my panicked body. I caught a glimpse of my pursuer with lucid desperation in their deep black eyes. I ducked and dived through the hollow trees and low hanging branches with finesse. Meanwhile, my new-found follower was crashing through said trees with pure frustration in their grunts and growls that echoed shortly after. Soon, the beast couldn't take any more and fell to the ground. I got to live another day in this hellscape.

Caelan Hames (15)
St John Baptist CIW High School, Aberdare

The Ancient Secret

"It has to be here somewhere," someone said to the others but then, the ground started to shake and crack around us. I felt a platoon of fear hit me but then, it stopped. The quake revealed a hidden facility.
"Look down there!" Sean shouted to me. We headed in. When the entrance shut, we turned around and an alien ran away like prey running from a predator.
"Uh-oh," I whispered quietly. After some time wandering through the deadly traps, we found the alien, who knocked us out.
"Who are you?" it said, gently.

Aaron Sparrow (14)
St John Baptist CIW High School, Aberdare

Hunted By The Darkness

Through the endless, deep blue ocean, I glide effortlessly with the current. Slow, flowing movements, deep focused thoughts. I am a world traveller, the marks of my adventures written on every inch of my shell. The ocean is my home. I have seen many sea creatures come and go but there are new monsters that lurk in the deep, hunting all in their path. They are a blanket of darkness, suffocating the innocent. These monsters move like wind-driven clouds through the ocean, turning day into night as their darkness consumes all. I am a sea turtle hunted by plastic.

Amelia Phillips (12)
St John Baptist CIW High School, Aberdare

Criminals

It's not safe now they know! How did they find out that I killed the Sargent? Then, I hear sirens wail. My legs tighten and every breath feels like swallowing a batch of nails. Suddenly, they find me. I push someone off their bike and pedal for my life. Someone screams, "Commandor Wills, stop now or we will shoot you." *They will never catch me,* I think. I go over a hill but my legs can't take it anymore. I collapse.
Quickly, someone says, "Commander Wills, you're under arrest for the murder of Sargeant Wiggins."

Daffydd Walters (14)
St John Baptist CIW High School, Aberdare

The Visitor

Alarms ringing, lights blaring. A creature was aboard the ship. Crewman rushed to the escape pods, getting away from the vile creature. A man screamed as a spike landed in his chest. Behind him, a large scaley creature was bearing its fangs, biting deep into his skill as blood dripped onto the floor. All hope had been lost. Bodies scattered the floor. The creature was hungry for more. It dashed through the ship, looking for its prey. It turned a corner and screeched. There was a shadow in the distance. The creature charged at the shadow, fangs ready.

Tyson Wicks (13)
St John Baptist CIW High School, Aberdare

Hunted, Chased And Denied

I could hear the screaming of adults and children. Mutant humans, more commonly known as zombies, had broken out of their containment. The population was growing. This place was a heaven from the apocalypse but now it was a hellhole. The place was filled with zombie dogs, zombie cats and the more dangerous zombies! I was currently hiding in the food and weapons storage. Very convenient. Although I was living in a dream place, I had lost my parents. They got infected and I had to shoot them! I was the last one standing and must recreate this heaven...

Luke Amos (12)
St John Baptist CIW High School, Aberdare

What Did I Do...?

I'm being watched, I know I am but I can't do anything. I'm rooted to the spot. I can't move or speak or anything. Inside, I scream but its no use, I can't get out... Someone enters. I can't see who they are but they walk around me. Then, they sit right in front of me. "Do you know why you're here?" he whispers softly.
"No," I stutter.
"Well, think harder, child. Maybe you will remember." I think really hard, as hard as I can. Suddenly, it hits me. I remember now. They must know...

Evie Jarrett (12)
St John Baptist CIW High School, Aberdare

The Purge

11am, the siren rang. It was almost time. An hour until it happened... I was looking outside my window. Everyone was ready. The streets were abandoned, like a ghost town. It was beginning in five minutes. We were ready. I heard screaming from across the street and gunfire. There it was, the siren was beginning now. Everyone had just gone crazy; guns were blazing and cars were racing. No one knew who was who... We had locked the house. We were armed and ready for anything that came our way. But we were not expecting something like this to happen...

Jack Davies (13)
St John Baptist CIW High School, Aberdare

The Search...

I could feel the blood dripping from my face. My fingers traced its worn and scarred skin. Every step was agonising. I couldn't run for much longer but I had to get away... I opened my eyes, oblivious to what was happening, a hot breath on my face. I quickly got onto my aching, bloody elbows and realised my face was bandaged...
"Be calm, 7143, I'm one of you..." the voice breathed quietly as it picked me up over its shoulder. So many thoughts sped through my brain. *Who was this person? And where was it taking me?*

Jade Stammers (12)
St John Baptist CIW High School, Aberdare

Not This Time...

"It's not safe here. I have to go!"
As I turned my head, a bony hand grabbed my shoulder.
"You're not going anywhere."
I screamed as loud as possible and ran for my life. I ran as fast as a cheetah. Dodging every piece of broken glass, I tried to run for safety. My muscles ached and my vision was going blurry. I looked up to see there was no end to this place. I kept running and running. I lost my balance and fell on a cold, wet floor.
"Where am I?" On no, not again. Not this time...

Tia Rhianne Sandhu (15)
St John Baptist CIW High School, Aberdare

The Intense Getaway!

I can't run for much longer. I am being hunted by the police. I'm scared the reason why I'm being hunted is that I have killed many people that were innocent. I wish I could change my past. The police are right behind me. I'm worried. There is a police car blocking me off. I don't hit the car. I'm speeding at 200mph, they're going at 179mph. I've nearly lost them. The SWAT team show up and shoot my tire and mirror. The bullet nearly hits my head. I have a heart attack. A car hits my side and *bang!*

Alex Jones (14)
St John Baptist CIW High School, Aberdare

Was It Really A Dream?

I stopped and looked, silence was screaming. The only light I had was the moon above. All was well. My fear was wearing out until I saw someone in the distance and heard a deafening shout. *He's back again, hungry for more*. I bolted it out, tree to tree, hoping he wouldn't be able to find me. After hours of running, climbing and sweating, I think I finally lost him. Relief filled me, I survived the zombie apocalypse. If only I could get out and be here no more! I heard someone calling me, was it really all a dream?

Gracie-May Owen
St John Baptist CIW High School, Aberdare

Wrong Turn

For a while, I thought it had stopped, but then I could hear it. My heart was thumping, my legs were burning from running so far. I could hear chimes whispering in the wind. It was evening in spring, getting darker and darker. Suddenly, car headlights lit up my fair skin. Some tall human was approaching me. Carefully, I stepped back. I could feel something cut my foot. The air turned black around me. I turned around, only hearing footsteps in the trees. Without a doubt, I knew I had to run for it. I screamed and could see something...

Isabelle Jones (11)
St John Baptist CIW High School, Aberdare

Escape, I Don't Think So

The sirens wailed as the only person I trust got shot. We were trying to escape a prisoner of war camp in Iraq. The person who got shot was my brother, Andrew. We both joined the armed forces together. We went to war and our squadron got captured and killed, all except me and Andrew, since we were the youngest. The day we got captured, me and Andrew were already thinking up a plan to escape.
Tonight, we've avoided all the obstacles except one. It was the fence - ten-foot high, then the guards were alerted then Andrew got shot.

Alexander Morgan (12)
St John Baptist CIW High School, Aberdare

Lost, Chased And Hunted

Hunted. That's what I was. *I didn't mean to do it,* I thought as I sprinted through the woods. Sirens wailed, loud police dogs barked... It wasn't safe for me here. I wasn't proud of what I did but I had to do it. It wasn't long before I reached a river. Shouts of officers and the roar of sirens were getting louder. I splashed through the murky waters until a strange flying machine arrived. I froze. "Put your hands up," someone shouted. I was... afraid. It was an accident. After all, I had never been to this planet before.

Ruby Tyler (12)

St John Baptist CIW High School, Aberdare

Hunted, Alone And Hostage

I looked down at my colourless, withered hands securely tied with a blood-spotted bandage, restraining me so I'm unable to escape from their brutal, merciless hands. Blinded by the lights, I could scarcely work out the faces of the ones I once loved. When I was naive and unable to see the grave danger I was in, and when these faces I did not wish to see were the faces of my dearest mother and father. Only then I realised how helpless and vulnerable I was. Only then I realised they were the hunters and I was the useless prey...

Aaliyah Morris (12)
St John Baptist CIW High School, Aberdare

The Hunted

I had thirty minutes to reach the border of Mexico; the purge was beginning! I was once the predator in the army but now I was the prey. The siren started, there were fifteen minutes! I was ten miles from the border. There was no one around. I was driving a truck, a Porsche 918 in matte black for emergencies. I picked up my friend. He was being attacked! "Are you okay, Steve?" I asked curiously.
"No," said Steve sobbing.
It had started. People were running outside. All you could hear were gunshots! We made it to Mexico!

Cameron Cresswell (12)
St John Baptist CIW High School, Aberdare

The Chase

Running faster and faster, my head pounding, blood pumping and adrenaline racing. Who were they? My feet and legs were pierced by the thorns and rocks in the dull, barren wasteland. I couldn't see their faces. I didn't dare look back. They were howling and wailing like a pack of angry animals. I could see it, my only hope. There was a canyon in front of me. I thought I might be able to jump off the edge down into the water below. I got closer and closer, then I jumped, tossing and turning down into the water and then...

Joseph Jones
St John Baptist CIW High School, Aberdare

Alien Hunt

The ship flew out of the water straight into a tower block and then several metal cubes fell from the sky! These things came out... I ran! Then a massive wave of energy knocked everyone off their feet. I blacked out. I woke up in a room with a glowing square for a door. I threw a screw. It bounced off it! I was prisoner! Suddenly, a wall collapsed. I was pulled through! Later, I heard, "Prisoner 2149872 has escaped!"
Then I heard, "Come here!" I turned. I was face to face with an alien! I cried out...

Zach Siddley (11)
St John Baptist CIW High School, Aberdare

It's The End

One day down at the zoo, there was one giraffe and one zebra. They were planning to go and escape. They were sick and tired of getting stuck in enclosed spaces all day, every day. So, they saw an escape route... As they ran like the wind out of that horrible place, as worker saw them. He pressed the alarm button. The siren started and all the zoo workers fled towards the gate and as they were running, they came across a massive creature, long, spikey and scary-looking. They both stopped, the workers caught up. It was the end.

Katie Toghill (12)
St John Baptist CIW High School, Aberdare

Alien Mansion Hunt

We were terrified and on the move. As we crept around the haunted mansion, as the children called it, we were fearing for our lives as the alien pursued us. All the law enforcers in the area were asleep and the army base nearby was under attack. As the bell chimed for twelve, we heard a blood-curdling scream and then an explosion. After our ears recovered from the blast, we realised our eldest brother, Geoff, was gone! As Barry went to go find him, we tried finding the alien. We discovered that it could teleport away from us.

Joshua Morgan (11)
St John Baptist CIW High School, Aberdare

Hunted - The Bizarre Discovery

Larry was hunting for animals in the spine-tingling forest. A few steps into the sinister forest and it suddenly went silent. He then heard a big snap. Larry looked over his shoulder and saw the colossal tree, then he took a closer look and saw a pair of abnormal eyes in the hole of the tree. The peculiar eyes blinked at Larry, who was frozen because he was so petrified. The eyes then completely disappeared. Once the eyes had vanished, Larry walked away. Whilst walking away, he immediately thought, *is it really true?*

Phoebe Sizer-Hancock (12)
St John Baptist CIW High School, Aberdare

The Mimic

Screaming is coming from all around, death and pain are all I know. All this, working for this confidential facility only to end up getting hunted. I help contain dangerous creatures, unknown by any average human. Creature 2046X, also known as The Mimic, has broken free. Its true form is a humanoid, body dark as a shadow with arms longer than its legs. This monster is able to shape-shift. It is chasing me down the dark hallway. I hear something all around me. I see a little girl and at that moment, I realise it is The Mimic.

Hudson Griffiths (11)
St John Baptist CIW High School, Aberdare

Run For My Life

This is the story where I'm going to tell you how I died. Let's take it back to 1891, January 5th. I walked past Wickory Woods as I heard footsteps following behind me... I took a detour. Wickory Woods is the creepiest around. The crows were never silent. At least until after I heard a *bang!* A bang that changed me. I was no longer in Wickory Woods. I could no longer move. I was dead. And I could never forget that traumatising and frightening experience! Little did I know how much somebody wanted me dead...

Ellie Louise Thomas
St John Baptist CIW High School, Aberdare

Kip's Story

Hi. My name is Kip, I'm a snow leopard. I've been separated from my family for three years. When I was young, my father was shot. My mother tried to hide me but it was too late, they were in the den. They shot my mother and screamed, "Where's the cub?" They were searching for hours. I stayed put, hoping that they would go away. It was twilight. I couldn't take it anymore. I decided to run, run for my life. I was spotted and shot in my left ear. I've been hunted all my life. Help, please...

Liberty Hetherington (12)
St John Baptist CIW High School, Aberdare

The Girl

It all started a year ago. The girl you used to know with hope and wonder in her eyes is gone. That warm-hearted girl now has a heart of stone. She is all alone. Lost. She's being chased by her own living demon. It's getting harder to convince herself she means something. She can't run much longer; she's running out of breath. It's going to catch her. She can't let that happen. She can't commit suicide; that's not the way she wants to die. She has changed forever. Or, so she thought. She had no idea what was to come.

Summer Williams (13)
St John Baptist CIW High School, Aberdare

The Great Hunt

There in its natural habitat was a wild caribou, but in the bush was a wild Australian hunter. He raised his barrel, looked down the scope and took aim. But suddenly, the caribou looked at him and ran off, but he was not going to give up. He followed it deeper into the forest. Then it came into view. He looked down the scope and pulled the trigger. He missed! "How could I miss?" he said to himself. Then something came up behind him. Something big, black and scary was the predator, and now he was the prey...

Jacob Catlow (12)
St John Baptist CIW High School, Aberdare

Don't Stop Running

I was running faster than the wind. My throat felt like fire. Blood dripped from my wounded arm until I dropped to the ground and rolled up against a tree that gave a sharp pain in my back. It had found me. The bloodthirsty creature began to drag my aching body into the trees. The vicious creature had a skeleton-like figure and razor-sharp teeth that had caused the unstoppable bleeding to my right arm. At this moment in time, my vision began to blur and all of a sudden, we'd stopped moving. I began to see light...

Charlotte Flaherty (12)
St John Baptist CIW High School, Aberdare

Demon In Disguise

My eyes flicker open. I'm trapped, tired and terrified. I am exactly where he wants me to be but I can't be here. I see a lock on the door, take a bobby pin out of my hair and begin to pick at it. He knows me but not my tricks. I escape outside and see a flashlight heading towards me. He's coming. I run, heading towards sheer darkness, escaping the demon in disguise, my feet ruined from twigs and fallen branches in this haunted wood. I'm still running but his footsteps get louder and louder and louder. "Help!"

Ella Moseley (14)
St John Baptist CIW High School, Aberdare

Hunted

I was muddy from head to toe. Running desperately to get away from the horrid building that I had been locked up in for maybe the whole of my life. I hated it there.
I had played together with my sister up until the unfortunate accident. That was when I was taken to that horrid grey building without my beloved sister. We were only four when it happened. Screaming, crying, thrashing... They would not leave me with my mother. She sent me there. She didn't want me back. There was something wrong with me...

Lucy Wright (11)
St John Baptist CIW High School, Aberdare

The Predators

Creak! I woke up. I looked around me, nothing. The next minute, the floor opened underneath me. I looked in awe as a ten-foot cave troll roared. I stood up. My first instinct was to run. Luckily, it was quite slow. I ran and ran through the dark, damp tunnel and caves. The sound of the troll slowly became quieter and quieter. I turned a corner. Suddenly, there was a tug on my leg. I turned around to see the horror of thirty ruthless goblins. My heart stopped and my whole life flashed before my eyes.

Dylan Brown (14)
St John Baptist CIW High School, Aberdare

Don't Move

The creature was gaining speed, leaping from tree to tree with its decomposing limbs. Its face was thin and hollow, as if no life behind its sunken eye sockets. It gripped its long talons into the mud as it landed in front of me, the same claws it had used to tear off my foot. I attempted to stay as still as possible, praying it would camouflage me but it could smell the dripping blood from my leg. It pounced on me with a high-pitched screech and intense pain flooded my body as it viciously tore at my flesh.

Rosie Blinkhorn (12)
St John Baptist CIW High School, Aberdare

The Predator's Howl!

I couldn't run for much longer. I heard a big howl from behind. I saw a shadow through the trees. Was this a dream? My head slowly turned to hear a colossal bang. My heart sank to the bottom of my stomach. I thought I would soon be in the stomach of my predator, stuck in a revolting world of slime. Was this how I meet my end? I hid quietly behind a massive oak tree, watching and hoping that I wasn't being followed. Then, I caught sight of two piercing brown eyes fixed on me. The most beautiful stag!

Mika-Leigh Ashley-Marsh
St John Baptist CIW High School, Aberdare

Running...

I have finally escaped the house with my life but not with my freedom. Sirens blare in my ears as I hear people running closer behind me with a furious look on their faces. I, however, have to run and keep on running. I feel water tricking off my face on to the ground. But these aren't raindrops. No. These are tears flowing from my eyes like a waterfall. My mind tells me to keep moving although my heart tells me to never forgive myself and to let them punish me. I've got to keep moving. I am being hunted.

Jake Glover (13)
St John Baptist CIW High School, Aberdare

How It All Changed

We were in the trenches when it happened, when we died. It just never stopped, the war seemed endless to us. Explosion after explosion, gunshot after gunshot, it just kept on going. It was then that I realised I might not make it. Then I saw a bomb falling rapidly from the sky, so I took cover. But he didn't. His name was Private Williams and he was my best friend. Me and him had lots of memories together. When the bomb landed, they all flashed before me. It took me a moment to realise he was gone...

Dylan Draper (13)
St John Baptist CIW High School, Aberdare

Escaping

I didn't mean to kill her. Honestly, I didn't but it's done now. I can't go back. I feel so bad, you don't understand. She was my friend, well, I thought she was but she betrayed me and you wouldn't have have been able to understand my anger. Now I just want to escape but there's no way out of this place. There are guards on watch all the time. They take you to dinner and even take you to the toilet! It's so strict.
I was an innocent person before, but sometimes anger can get the best of you.

Isabelle Jacklin (11)
St John Baptist CIW High School, Aberdare

The Park On Mulberry Lane

It was this night, we had to run for our lives! It was a cold night, me and my best friend, Gracie, were hanging out in the park. We were enjoying our time when the sky went dark, like something was looming over us. Then, out of the trees, a dark shadow appeared, then another one, and another...
Gracie turned to me and said, "Should we go home now?"
It was all a blur. We were being chased and then darkness. We were thrown into a van and neither of us knew exactly what was in store...

Emma Lacey (12)
St John Baptist CIW High School, Aberdare

The Chase

They were everywhere. It was the whole police force against me. They had been trying to catch me for years and finally, they had their chance. The sirens were wailing in the background as I was racing through the city. I was swerving all over the place. One thing that scared me the most was being cornered and knowing there was no way to escape. "Argh!" They were getting closer and I could feel the car giving up on me. My fear had come true, I was cornered. It was the end. My run was over. But, then...

Tristan Skelton (15)
St John Baptist CIW High School, Aberdare

School Lockdown!

I was hiding in the computer room, clutching my knees as if I was holding on for dear life. The only thing I could hear was the alarm, the alarm for lockdown. I jumped when someone on the tannoy said, "Keep the doors locked shut. If you see a man with a black hoodie and grey trousers, run the opposite way. Keep safe before he-" It stopped. I was now texting my friend and she asked where I was. I said the computer room. She stopped texting! I was panicking so much. I heard a bang, it was him!

Macy Lyla Burns (11)
St John Baptist CIW High School, Aberdare

The Real Nightmare

It was like a nightmare. I began to run faster and faster but I could never get away from him, no matter how fast I went. But, I couldn't wake up from this. This was reality. I was getting chased. My legs began to ache and I started to slow down. I could hear him breathe, loud and clear. Hopefully, he was tired too. Hopefully, he'd give up. I heard his footsteps disappear and I stopped running to let out of sigh of relief. But then, I turned around. He was there. We were face to face... I was doomed.

Rebekah Williams (15)
St John Baptist CIW High School, Aberdare

The Gas Attack

One day, I was running from a bright, lime-green gas. Then suddenly, I heard someone screaming, "Someone help me!" He had lost his gas mask, I didn't know what to do. So, I turned back and tried dragging him away from the gas but it was too late. He was already dead. I couldn't help him anymore. Even though I didn't know who he was, I still felt bad. I couldn't keep on dragging him, he was getting heavier and heavier each minute. So, I left him dead, lying down in a ditch.

Erin Jones (13)

St John Baptist CIW High School, Aberdare

The Tears I Cry...

Running through the broken trees, the raindrops soak the sky. Are they raindrops? No, they aren't, they're the tears I'm crying. I look around. Which way to go? I turn around for a way to escape, an opening in the trees! I make my way. The trees are clawing my arms as I sprint and the thorns are stinging my legs! I run faster until I simply can't anymore. My heart is telling me to stop running but I know I can't for I'm a bad person. A person being hunted with no escape. I am wanted, I am hunted.

Catrin Howells (12)
St John Baptist CIW High School, Aberdare

In The Woods

The sirens started in the woods. They were looking for the body. Me and my friend were in the woods at that time when suddenly, my friend's dad, who was a police officer, found my friend in the woods at night. But I hid behind a tree.
About five minutes later, I was on my own. It was pitch-black and I couldn't see a thing. *Crack!* I twisted my ankle and fell down a hill. Suddenly, I found the dead body. It was full of bite marks. I turned my torch on, then I discovered a werewolf...

Grace Driscoll (12)
St John Baptist CIW High School, Aberdare

Last Stand

"Gas. Gas! Quick boys, put on these masks." The Germans had found us and now it was a game of cat and mouse. We were the mice and the Germans were the cats slowly hunting us down. We were being killed and were slowly being outnumbered, we ran to our trenches to life and try to recover. However, the cats found us and opened fire. They came at us with all their anger and we slowly started to realise how this was going to end up if we didn't do anything and just hid in our trenches.

Jay Bishop (13)
St John Baptist CIW High School, Aberdare

Mysterious Woods

I walked into the forest with my friend. We walked for one hour and then we sat down for a picnic. I went to the river to get water. I got back to the table and my friend wasn't there. I shouted for her but couldn't hear anything. It was silent. I pulled my phone out to call the police but there wasn't a signal. I heard a noise that I thought was my friend. I looked behind me and saw a monster. I screamed loud so the world could hear. I looked into its big, creepy, moonlit eyes...

Carys Crellin (13)
St John Baptist CIW High School, Aberdare

Childhood Nightmare!

My whole body was trembling in fear as he chased me through my childhood school. I knew the only option I had left was to run outside and hope I was faster than him. I didn't recognise him. All I saw was his run-down and burned face. *Smash!* That was him! I hear him dragging his saw across the wall and hear the blood dripping onto the floor. I've decided! I'm legging it! My heart was racing like it was in the Grand Prix, knowing that this could be the end. I looked back, he was gone.

Lewis Jones (14)
St John Baptist CIW High School, Aberdare

The Dark Figure

It was getting dark, it was still chasing me. I didn't know what to do except run away from it. All of a sudden, it stopped. I had a chance to hide. My whole body was shivering and it felt like I was being stabbed because I'd run so far. It looked like a black figure with red ghoulish eyes that went through me. It started chasing me again, but I couldn't run, my legs were as stiff as a brick. I felt like a statue. *Goodbye!* I thought as it appeared right in front of me...

Tylor Sweet (11)
St John Baptist CIW High School, Aberdare

The Runaway

I've become the prey. I only killed two allies, however, the police are hunting for me. At this moment, I am hiding in a sewer. It smells but it's worth it. They have dogs and hundreds of police officers after me. I have to move. They are nearby. I run quickly to the nearest drain above me. I have to hide. Officers enter the sewer and I run and hide behind a wall. They go past, they don't see me. To get to the drain, above me, I have to climb up. I do. I am surrounded by police.

Iestyn Donovan (12)
St John Baptist CIW High School, Aberdare

The Cub...

My name is Joey. I am a jaguar cub and I'm not safe where I am. I lost my mother while learning to hunt. That was when the predator became the prey. Let me explain. I was learning to hunt so that when I am older, I can find my own food. Then they came. Some spiteful men shot my mother with a dart and she fell asleep. They yelled, "Get the cub!" They were coming after me! I ran for my life until I couldn't hear or see them anymore. I was lost and afraid. I was being hunted!

Bethany Shepherd (12)
St John Baptist CIW High School, Aberdare

The Big Bad 'Wolf'

I continued to walk, gun in hand. I was the predator now and the beast that stole Savannah's life was the prey. I could hear her crying ringing in my head. I held onto the gun tighter, fear in my heart but not in my head. "Come out, you beast!" I let out a cry. I could hear its paws but no animals were in sight. "Savannah did not deserve to die! You do and you will!" I looked around, waiting for a response. Nothing happened. All of a sudden, I got lifted into the air. My breathing slowed...

Phoebe Phillips (11)
St John Baptist CIW High School, Aberdare

Alien Undercover

I could not run for much longer. My chest was hurting now and they knew where I was, they knew what I was! I tried to run back to the spaceship but I couldn't. The people on Earth were hunting for me and I couldn't do anything about it. I realised I had a tracker on my arm, they had been able to see me the whole time! I grabbed my arm, pulled the tracker off and started running again. I had become the prey a while after I started moving. I was closer to the spaceship. Please help...

Chloe Toop (11)
St John Baptist CIW High School, Aberdare

I Couldn't Run

It's not safe now they know what I am. I hear lasers everywhere. I think, I really hope they don't find me. I really don't want them to find me. It's like I'm in a trap all alone, nowhere to go because I know wherever I go is going to be a mistake. I know I'm not going to be left alone, I'm stuck in a scary, damp forest. I keep hearing footsteps, I also hear owls but then, I suddenly stop. I think I've lost the footsteps. I can't move. I can't run...

Amy Lee Smith (11)
St John Baptist CIW High School, Aberdare

Scary Moment

I just woke up to the sound of sirens. As I moved slowly and steadily in the darkness towards the door, I heard a horrific sound that came out of nowhere as if someone was being murdered. I opened the door and I saw a shadow in the distance of someone running. The only thing I could hear was the footsteps getting faster and faster in the distance. I crept slowly out. It was silent. Then, I heard a noise behind me. I started running faster and faster. I was scared. Where was I going to go?

Lauren Jex (11)

St John Baptist CIW High School, Aberdare

Hunted In A Hospital

I couldn't run for much longer, I didn't know who was chasing me but I knew I wasn't safe. I saw a hospital and climbed through a window. I locked myself in a room and heard a noise. "Hello?" I said.
"It's me, Theo. Run," he said, "and don't look them in the eye."
We ran down a corridor, light flickering all around us. "Run faster Ashton!"
"I can't!" I collapsed on the floor and then it grabbed me. "Argh!"
I woke up. What a dream... I heard a siren. Was it a dream...?

Ashton Bow (11)
St John Baptist CIW High School, Aberdare

The Hunted School House

I arrived at Baldi's schoolhouse. The halls were empty. I was searching to find any survivors. I opened the door into a classroom and I found Baldi. I asked him what was going on. Baldi told me that he was getting hunted by Sonic E X. We were close to the entrance. The chase was hopeless, we thought that we were going to die there. We made it out of the schoolhouse. We got onto the school bus. We got away from him as I threw dynamite into the schoolhouse. It blew up into smithereens.

Thiago Lima Westwood (14)
St John Baptist CIW High School, Aberdare

Prison Escape

I couldn't run any longer. The sirens were wailing, my legs were aching and I just wanted to disappear. Where could I go? I was running for almost an hour and I still had nowhere to hide. Soon, they would find me. I'd be the prey and get caught. It wasn't safe out here. I could hear wolves howling in the distance and movement from behind trees. I just wanted to be home. After doing more walking, I came across a hut. It was a relief when I saw it but I walked inside and saw the police...

Evie Manning (12)
St John Baptist CIW High School, Aberdare

The Failed Experiment

It wasn't safe now they knew I was a mutant able to morph any part of my body into anything. I could even become someone else. My mission was to stop them, stop the people at the lab from making more mutants like me. I originally was the perfect creature but I went rogue and now I was considered a failed experiment. As far as I knew, I was the only one it worked on. All the others were monsters. On my path, I would demolish anyone or anything in my way. Destroying HEAR was my goal...

Carwyn Evans (13)
St John Baptist CIW High School, Aberdare

Stuck In A Bag!

I couldn't run for much longer. The prey was getting further and further away. All I could hear were sirens ringing in my head. I looked in the distance to see that the prey had suddenly stopped. I edged closer to the prey and it moved a step ahead. I wondered what it could be as I took a step closer again. I still couldn't quite see what this prey was. There was no movement at all so I kept edging closer and closer, I was now standing right beside the prey. I looked over...

Thea Lloyd (12)
St John Baptist CIW High School, Aberdare

A Run For Life

I race through the cobbled streets as fast as my bloody legs will take me. My vision goes fuzzy and my legs feel like they will snap at any second. I hear him getting closer. His footsteps echo in my ears and I feel the leather belt against the backs of my legs. My body feels like it's burning on a bonfire. I reach down at my legs in agony and blood seeps through my fingers. I stumble onto my knees and pull myself up with all my strength. I need to get away... for my baby.

Abigail Chidgey (13)
St John Baptist CIW High School, Aberdare

Death Wood!

I had twenty-four hours to escape. I was chained to a table. I tried to escape but then... he woke up. I snapped my ankle with blood everywhere. I jumped out the window to find everyone I knew dead in the front garden, scattered everywhere. I wanted to cry at what I saw. My husband lay dead on the lawn. He had an axe in his head. I started limping as fast as I could. I ran to the border of the forest, but then I saw him standing there in black, waiting for me to run away.

Seren Sanderson (12)
St John Baptist CIW High School, Aberdare

Just A Dream

I had twenty-four hours... I was in darkness, trapped, with only one way out and I had to make a run for it. There was one thing in my way, the gigantic gash that was carved deep into my stomach. That wasn't enough to stop me so I ran for it. I mean I tried to but the sharp pain coming from my wound was unbearable. However, I powered through it and I made it out the door. I was free at last! I heard shouting from afar so I opened my eyes and realised it was all a dream.

Gracie Williams (12)
St John Baptist CIW High School, Aberdare

The Chase

I sat as I stared at the dark and starry sky. I wondered why this thing was after me, why I had to run away from it for hours in the woods. Then I heard the all-too familiar thumping sound coming faster and faster. I gathered my stuff and ran for it. I knew I had to make a plan and quickly. I ran into the tall grass and saw it getting further away. I found a small cottage and created my plan. I made a fake me, coated it with its favourite smell... I was safe... for now.

Ava-Lucia Warren (11)
St John Baptist CIW High School, Aberdare

Who Is It?

I'm not safe anymore. He knows exactly where I am. My heart is pounding like it is about to burst out of my chest. I'm in a broken down, abandoned shed when I hear a familiar voice saying, "Ready or not, here I come." I take a look to see if I can escape. I see a long, skinny shadow staring right back at me. It feels as if I have needles in my throat. I hear heavy breathing behind me. I shiver with panic. I turn around with a sign of relief. A face that I've missed...

Ella Jones (11)

St John Baptist CIW High School, Aberdare

Hunting The Prey

We are at war. It is horrible because we are fighting against people. We are getting shot at. It is our job to hunt the enemy. We are a team of snipers and we see straight into the eyes of the Germans. We find it hard to shoot at them because we can see them. We shoot at a man and his head splatted off like a tomato. It's likely that we are going to die in the war. It will be horrible to go home after seeing all of this. It makes me upset seeing myself like this.

Thomas Walters (13)
St John Baptist CIW High School, Aberdare

The Great War

Bang! The gas was coming towards us, it was green and thick. We ran for our lives. All we heard was a bang like an explosion. Everybody was screaming and falling to the ground. We quickly put our masks on. We tried to run, our bags were heavy. Some fell to the ground just before they put their masks on. We couldn't see. It was too thick to see anything. I saw someone coming towards me. It was the enemy coming. I grabbed my gun and he fell to the ground.

Libby Johns (13)
St John Baptist CIW High School, Aberdare

A Death In The Moonlight

The hunt was on. The blood was pumping, my heart was racing. I was in trouble. They were about to catch me. I could hear them but I had to keep going. My head bleeding now, if I stopped they would soon find me. I looked around. I was surrounded by trees and there they were. I was well and truly finished. But then, in the corner of my eye, I saw a glint in the moonlight. It was a small metal pole. As they got out their shiny knives, I leaned down to grab the pole...

Freddie Rickards (12)
St John Baptist CIW High School, Aberdare

On The Run!

I didn't mean to kill her! I really didn't mean to. I am sorry but it's done now. I can't run for much longer. I have been running for days. If I don't escape the country, I am going to prison. I hear the sirens wailing, I know they are close. I am running like the wind through the grass and over logs. I run onto the path. I can see the helicopter now. It is just a field away. Then, the sirens catch up with me. They see me... I wake up. It was just a dream!

Anja Bennett (11)
St John Baptist CIW High School, Aberdare

On The Run!

The siren started as soon as I robbed the bank. I was a criminal! The siren was ringing very loudly. It wasn't safe now, they were coming for me. I was running for more than thirty minutes. I couldn't run any longer. My legs were hurting. I couldn't stop now, they were catching up! I was gonna run into the forest and climb up a tree and hide the money, but then I saw flashing torches. They knew where I was. They were coming towards me...

Lauren Davies (13)
St John Baptist CIW High School, Aberdare

Hunted

I couldn't run for much longer, my legs were slowly giving up on me. As I looked to the right of me, I saw it! Then, it was gone. I looked to the left and it was there again! I didn't want to give up but my body thought another thing. My legs gave way and I collapsed to the floor. I knew it was over now. I could hear its footsteps creeping up on me and then, I heard it behind me. It was closing in on me. I knew it was over now. I'd been hunted.

Lincoln Hall (12)
St John Baptist CIW High School, Aberdare

The Cottage

I couldn't run for my life much longer. I found a little cottage in the middle of the woods, this cottage looked derelict. I walked into the cottage and there were men looking at my feet. My feet were black, on the other hand, my nose was like an iceberg. I had pines and needles everywhere. I walked inside and I had a cold shiver. They moved right in front of me. They slammed the door shut and they tried to shoot me...

Madison Shellard (11)
St John Baptist CIW High School, Aberdare

The Chase

It is not safe now they now what I am. They are gonna chase me and kill me. I am scared to death. What will they do to me?
I run to hide and keep myself safe, but I don't know how because they are nasty people.
I am called Amelia and I am 6'5" feet tall and I am purple and red. I am an alien, but some people think I am human, but I am not, so what should I do now?

Emmy Serpell (12)
St John Baptist CIW High School, Aberdare

Hunted

My body, consumed in terror that I will never see outside my own fear. The darkness is only broken by the small rays of light seeping through the canopy of the trees. Mist covers everything, only a few close trees are visible. Everything is silent apart from a few birds singing happily as if their lives were perfect. I can't hear them, I can't see them, but there is a feeling in the back of my mind that they're there, watching me, waiting until I am vulnerable. I hear a gunshot. They're here...

William Morris
Stoke College, Stoke By Clare

Hunted

It has been days, days of torture, torture that seems to be unending. The fear of seeing them again flows through me, through my veins. It terrorises me as I sleep as the dark night encloses around it in its continuous gloom. My body is consumed in horror that one day, they will find me and I will never see outside my own worries.
However far I may run from them, there is always that feeling that thought that they are there. They are watching me, stalking my every move. I am being hunted...

Kieran Vickers
Stoke College, Stoke By Clare

Hunted

I can't shake this feeling that I'm being hunted. I can't see the trees, yet I feel like I can hear them. Since I've become blind, my other senses have heightened; I feel the breeze of the birds flying past and I can hear the buzzing of the bees in their hive. I feel that there is someone watching me, staring at me, and, I freeze. I suddenly have a chilling touch of air come to me. I want to relax for once, but I always feel this stressing feeling... that comforts me...

Alfie Cameron (13)
Stoke College, Stoke By Clare

Breathe

"I have to escape, now," I told myself, the echoing sirens drilled into my skull as my feet trudged into the murky depths of the mud. My bag flailing around behind me as I shrugged it off. Useless. I then encountered a street, tiles ripped apart and overgrowth surrounding the bricks. Down the street, left, right, down, here! The wind stroked my cheek, a constant distraction to my longing for life as a gurgling noise invaded the surrounding ambience and dark shadows. I ran straight to the end of the road. Crawling back, struggling for breath, I fell over...

Ellis Joseph Blake (13)
The Astley Cooper School, Hemel Hempstead

Prey

Sirens wailed. Fresh blood dripped down my chin. I shouldn't have done it yet my inner demon praised me. I yearned for more though felt disgusted by my own vile thoughts. The moment blurred but I became a monster in the eyes of the village, and to myself, as soon as the body was lifeless beneath me. A body without a conscience which had saved mine. The twisted realisation of it all took a dreadful grip. I tried to flee but the light radiating from the torches tainted me. I felt the heat burn my body, licking my soul.

Sarita Silwal (13)
The Astley Cooper School, Hemel Hempstead

I'm So Sorry

I had twenty-four hours to live. I was hunted by my own self-doubt. I had nothing left: my girlfriend, now ex-girlfriend, took everything important with her. As a tear dropped onto the letter that I clutched tightly in my palms, everything went dull. I stopped crying and my mind went blank. Twenty-four hours turned to five in what seemed like minutes. Everything was set up, I had sent messages to everyone I once cared for. Two minutes left. I stood on the stool with no emotion. It was all over. I'm so sorry...

Jessica Lyn Waite (14)
The Astley Cooper School, Hemel Hempstead

Help Me...

I had twenty-four hours to live or die, but why would they hunt me My friend chopped people's heads off, stole candy and even murdered children but they framed me. The people would never believe me. I hid in an abandoned house. I heard the door break. I tried to not scream or even shout for help. I heard footsteps getting closer and closer so I ran faster than the person. I looked back, he had a gun. I kept running until I fell. He was close. "Goodbye," the person mumbled as he shot me...

Samantha-Jane Price (11)
The Astley Cooper School, Hemel Hempstead

It Was Here

I had to leave, now. Someone, no, something was coming. A blood-curdling roar made my heart skip a beat. Suddenly, I couldn't breathe, I felt like I was being choked. Then, I fell with a thud to the ground. I lay there, cuddled up, barely alive. I could see it now. Once I saw it, I wouldn't be able to erase it from my memory. The adrenaline flew over my veins like a carp through a river. The absolute horror paralysed me. My life was about to end. I was picked up and blackness fell over me. I was dead.

Hyed Haq (11)
The Astley Cooper School, Hemel Hempstead

Colt Killing

I couldn't run for much longer, no-man's-land had been deserted but it sounded packed. Gunshots danced across no-man's-land as I dashed across the muddy, mucky, sticky ground. I didn't think I would make it. I lifted up my rifle and poised it, ready to fire. The cold air ran up my spine, this felt like it would be the end of the line for me. I could see the light already. I might as well crawl into a ball and wait for my end. I was ready. I said my last prayers...

Jamie Buckingham (12)
The Astley Cooper School, Hemel Hempstead

It's Not Safe

We were so close. At least until we weren't. I felt so powerless and can't do anything about what she does. All I can do is sit in a corner and cry. She was hunting me down. I can't run for long. Everyway is a dead end in the end. A dead end with walls too high to climb out and escape from. They always have me within their grasp; abusing me with more of their hate... No, evil words. Cutting me down to make their pedestal higher. They feed their ego off of me. I'm not safe, am I?

Amelia Edwards (14)
The Astley Cooper School, Hemel Hempstead

The Werewolf On Shadow Lake

We had to leave, now. The beast charged towards us at the speed of light, hopping over crooked trees and slashing people in the forest in its bloodthirsty path. We ran but we both knew one of us wasn't going to make it. Suddenly, I fell onto the rocky ground. I blacked out but, when I opened my eyes, my friend was gone, devoured by the werewolf of Shadow Lake, the cursed legend of Glastonbury.

Sean Hayes (12)
The Astley Cooper School, Hemel Hempstead

Internal Terror

Every day awake. Fear. Hunted. Again. Repeat. Hunted further, hunted deeper. My eyes physically not making out the 'creature' that stabbed me. Not physically, internally. My instinct sensing a deep hurt but my brain repelling that thought. Still relaxed on my cushioned bed, yet my legs felt as if they were racing, running from the 'creature'. The 'creature' was hungry. Hungry for something I did not know, what I did not see. I did not hear. Was it me? Was it my blood? Or something deeper with more meaning. Then one stab, one internal stab. Pain left me eternally.

Amel Djoudi (13)
Thomas Deacon Academy, Peterborough

Cornered

Walking slowly across the dense forest, out of breath, she dug her hands into her pockets, checking if she had her inestimable weapon. In the distance, she could hear sirens wail, deafening her ears. Heart beating, she didn't like the thought of her in a solitary, gloomy prison cell.
"Hey, get back here!"
She turned her head frantically to look back at the broad man pointing a gun at her. Agitated, she ran like a cheetah catching its prey. Breathing heavily, she took a halt and took a minute to breathe. A helicopter stopped above her. She felt cornered...

Afrida Nahar (12)
Thomas Deacon Academy, Peterborough

Just... Keep... Running

I was running so fast, I was putting lightning to shame. Darting through the trees, I glanced behind me and still saw three jet-black silhouettes gradually gaining on me. I was stumbling through the eerie forest, panting and gasping for even the slightest of breaths. Adrenaline pierced through my bloodstream and a fierce shiver shot down my spine. Leaves crunched under my every desperate step. I could still hear their raucous laughter ringing through the trees. They wanted me to be terrified but their laughter only fueled my aggression as I pounded my feet harder on the dirt.

Halwest Aziz (12)

Thomas Deacon Academy, Peterborough

Special Treasure

They had twenty-four hours to find something special. Max needed to collect timepieces to open a portal of time travelling. Max had to get riddles so he could collect all the pieces.
Little did he know, there was someone else who wanted the treasure - Marcus.
Three hours left. Max had nine out of ten timepieces. One hour, he had to get the last riddle.
Ten minutes, he found it. He had to put all the timepieces in a golden circle. The portal opened. He entered it.
Max was shivering with fear. He found it, he was victorious.

Alex Turlakov (11)
Thomas Deacon Academy, Peterborough

Hunted

Me and my crew were dashing away, sirens wailed through the streets. There wasn't anywhere to go.
"What are we going to do, boss?" Asked James.
The police surrounded us. Alex saw an open door and we all sprinted through as quickly as possible. They started opening fire and shot Alex in the back.
"Get up!" I told him. "Get up!"
They started shooting again and he was dead. Only the two of us now.
We ran upstairs and into an empty room. We didn't know what to do. We were being hunted.

Muhammed Junaid Malik (11)
Thomas Deacon Academy, Peterborough

The Creature

500 miles to the border. 500 miles to catch James. He limps slowly away and I jog, gaining fast. The scenery changes as darkness engulfs us. Rocks are nightmarish figures, James a lifeless heap. The chase is up. I move towards him, then I stop. A creature fills my vision. Ignoring the warnings filling my head, I do the worst thing possible: I run. The hunter is the hunted! Fear of the creature weighs me down. Pebbles become hurdles, rocks towering walls. The creature comes closer. It has won. I turn, see a gap, dive through it and run away.

Eloise Dobbing (12)
Thomas Deacon Academy, Peterborough

When You Hear A Splinter... Run

The crimson rose by my feet reminds me of the terror that haunts us. I hear a twig splinter (sharp and crisp) in the forest. I become stiff with paranoia, my mind spirals, my legs racing, my heart drumming and my breath a heavier weight. I don't blink until the strain becomes a burden, suddenly I'm in a field, a beautiful haven. Until I hear the footsteps and raspy breaths. Before I run, weeds capture me. Claws dig into my back... my eyes open. Was it my imagination? I turn to see a splintered twig. All I think is... *run.*

Aisha Ahmed (15)
Thomas Deacon Academy, Peterborough

Hunted

As Viki and Cami shut the door behind them, they heard something run quickly through the woods. They rushed to see what it was. They were too late. Bow and arrow in hands, they thought they would have something to eat. Viki and Cami started to walk back to their cottage but then the hopeless animal ran past them and with one fling, dead! As soon as they did, they heard sirens wailing throughout the whole village. Both of their hearts were pounding out of their chests. They just wanted a meal but they were getting hunted instead!

Emilija Jovkovska (11)
Thomas Deacon Academy, Peterborough

Seventy-Two Hours

I had seventy-two hours to hide. The hunters weren't far behind. They were searching. I knew they were. I could smell them. I couldn't run for much longer. Sirens wailed, echoing from the distant mountains behind me. I needed to hide in the tunnels. I needed to try and use my magic to create a diversion! Even though I was vomiting blood due to my fatigue, it was my only option. That was better than none. Seventy-two hours were coming to an end. The sirens came closer. That's when I knew I had been hunted.

Shniya Marie Kelly (11)
Thomas Deacon Academy, Peterborough

Sadness

They were here, always able to find me, but they should also know I am always one step ahead. It is one thing to run away from co-workers, but it is another to run away from the only family you've ever known. But all that didn't matter now. They needed it from me, they needed to die to obtain money and power. I inherited my money from my uncle, my last-known relative. I hated this vigilante lifestyle. I couldn't make any new friends, had to distance myself away from everyone, be on the run. It was very terrifying...

Arwa Jahangir (13)
Thomas Deacon Academy, Peterborough

The Last Of My Nightmares...?

Today was the night I had the last of my nightmares about Edward. You might think this was a good thing, but it wasn't... I was running towards a graveyard, chains being dragged behind me. Edward was chasing me, I was screaming... I heard someone call my name. I felt a hand touch my cheek. Hoping that it wasn't Edward, I slowly opened my eyes. Thankfully, it was my Emma, my BFF. I was waking out the front door when I saw Edward staring at me. So it wasn't a dream! As I turned around, I saw Edward...

Noor Ramzan (11)
Thomas Deacon Academy, Peterborough

The Free, The Bad And The Dirty

That sound broke me. Like a stone being thrown in a glass house. It killed my confidence, frothing at the mouth as if its one objective was to hunt. Me. Down. The eardrum-piercing howl shrouded me in darkness, corrupting my frail soul. The trees wailed, the leaves ripped and rustled and the beast groaned. I felt it approaching, I felt its hunger for meat, its thirst for blood. The smell of fresh air impaled me like tiny daggers. The snapping of mini twigs grew louder with every second. I just wanted to live.

Jacob Danaher (13)
Thomas Deacon Academy, Peterborough

The Run

The ground began to shake. At first no one moves, their brains unable to make sense of the input from their feet. The sound of extended thunder is rattling in my ears and like a switch has been flicked, everyone flights for safety! The dim lights flicker rapidly before going out and the table is pouncing like it has a mind of its own. The oaky, toxic smell of fire permeates the room and then I see it. A colossal, azure wave sweeping into the hectic city! A tsunami. I have to run but my legs refuse to move...

Wiktoria Apakitsa (13)
Thomas Deacon Academy, Peterborough

Shift

The body's right there. There, in front of me. I can hear them coming but won't move. My head's screaming at me to run. My feet move but I'm still there. That moment keeps on replaying over and over again. I burst through the doors and stumble into the envelope of the night. The shadows are drawing nearer. I quicken my pace but my head won't clear. Frantic steps are echoing behind me. I blindly stumble to the edge of the cliff. There's no time to think, they'll be here soon. I have to do something. I fall.

Alice Lyall (12)
Thomas Deacon Academy, Peterborough

Run For Your Life

I couldn't run for much longer. My lungs inhaled every last piece of breath before they became sore. Without thinking, I stumbled into a ditch.
I used all of my energy to lift myself out. Out before I was caught. They were coming. I dived into the ditch I fell in and held my breath.
All of a sudden, I heard loud footsteps. They were closer and ready to arrest. At that moment, I tripped and fell. The footsteps stopped.
The last thing I saw was two large figures, and then darkness.

Juweria Alam (12)
Thomas Deacon Academy, Peterborough

Safe?

"In here!" I wailed. We entered a huge field filled with bushes and trees.
"He could be anywhere," my friend, Delilah, exclaimed.
We heard rustling of leaves. "Ssh," I said.
"What was that?" Delilah asked.
"That doesn't matter, look!" I pointed at a bush. We rushed to it and reached inside.
There he was, my puppy, Cinnamon. We ran to a tiny cellar that was compacted with people.
We squeezed our minute bodies inside, relieved we were safe. At least for now.

Skaiste Sinusaite (12)
Thomas Deacon Academy, Peterborough

The Runaway And The Hunters

The things I've done for nothing. I've gone miles, removed the chip so I wouldn't join them. It was a fake. I gutted one so they couldn't smell me. I hosed myself with ice so they couldn't see me. I now have my hunters trying to destroy the building where I hide. Now my final fear is right above me. I delayed them. If you read this, they are coming for you. My end is here. Find the ship. My final goodbye is here. I cannot go further, but you can! I've been hunted...

Leon Martin Jordan Cartledge (11)
Thomas Deacon Academy, Peterborough

The Poaching

Imagine thinking about a nightmare that came to life.
Imagine life at its worst. This is my story.
I awoke from the screaming voices in my head and regretted what I did yesterday. Around 6pm, we were hunting for rabbits but we didn't know there was a criminal about. It was petrifying.
Suddenly, a torch shone on the rabbit and there was a gun pointing at us. We sprinted as far as we could, to the other side of town, in the dark! But we didn't expect this to happen...

Romeesa Raza (12)
Thomas Deacon Academy, Peterborough

A Shot Of Horror

Lonely and abandoned, a small hut lay lopsided, held up only by the foundations of greenery. I don't know how I got here but as soon as I adjusted to my surroundings, the serenity was broken by a loud gunshot! Or, that's what I thought it was. It was heard by the fauna nearby. Then another. I tried to run but the last one got me! I was helpless and all I could do was feel sorry for myself. My life seeped out of my body. A pitch-black figure came up to me. It raised its hand...

Owais Gaibee (11)

Thomas Deacon Academy, Peterborough

Maya

The infection started three days ago. That's funny, isn't it? I can't remember what my name is, or where I am. But I *can* remember when the soul-eating undead came to have some five-star gourmet human. One other thing I remember... Maya. I dunno who she is or why she's important, but there's something I need to know. Who is she and why is she stuck in my damn head? But before I can moan any more about how much my life sucks, I hear an ominous knock at the door...

Adam Cunnington (13)
Thomas Deacon Academy, Peterborough

Running In The Dark

I knew I couldn't run for much longer. Not to mention, I was running in the dark. It was wrong of them to hunt down such a harmless animal. I could still hear the guns shooting and the thudding of footsteps in the background. They were not going to stop until they found the animal. It seemed like they wanted me too, along with the animal. The cold wind blew against my face as I ran for my life. No one knew what they would do when they found me...

Mahnoor Malik (12)
Thomas Deacon Academy, Peterborough

The Hunted

A canon echoed in the dusty air. Another had been caught. I panicked. They wouldn't rest until the month's end or until they found every person that was left. My legs throbbed at the aching pain of running in circles in the middle of nowhere. I didn't want to think about what was going to happen if I was found. But I did. When I slept, when I ran, even when I was hunting animals for food. I already knew I was going to be hunted...

Thea Richmond (11)
Thomas Deacon Academy, Peterborough

Hunt Or Be Hunted

It all went wrong. Why did I sign up? Now I am running away, hoping they don't find me.
I'm gasping for air. I hear daunting screams of my mother being devoured by our own kind. I hear footsteps and the never-ending, blood-curdling screams of the innocent.
If somebody is reading this, don't sign up. Or you will end up like me, trapped in a cave, lost in the abyss. I am the prey and they are the predators.

Anwar Ali (12)
Thomas Deacon Academy, Peterborough

The Runner

We were nearly there. We knew that it was dangerous, however, we had to keep running. The mud squelched as we ran on it.
We entered the forest. The stitch in my side was a knife stabbing me. I felt like the trees were shaking their heads in shame.
I couldn't do it, I had to stop. But they were there...

Maryam Iraj Yaseen (11)
Thomas Deacon Academy, Peterborough

YOUNG WRITERS INFORMATION

We hope you have enjoyed reading this book – and that you will continue to in the coming years.

If you're a young writer who enjoys reading and creative writing, or the parent of an enthusiastic poet or story writer, do visit our website **www.youngwriters.co.uk**. Here you will find free competitions, workshops and games, as well as recommended reads, a poetry glossary and our blog. There's lots to keep budding writers motivated to write!

If you would like to order further copies of this book, or any of our other titles, then please give us a call or order via your online account.

Young Writers
Remus House
Coltsfoot Drive
Peterborough
PE2 9BF
(01733) 890066
info@youngwriters.co.uk